Feeding the
Dragon

Written by
John Townsend

Illustrated
by Dynamo

Shshsh …
It's back.
The dragon has returned and it's hungry.
Very hungry.

It's waiting to be fed at the top of the mountain – and it's angry.
Very angry.

If no one feeds it soon, it will swoop down and grab us in its terrible claws.
It will puff red smoke from its sizzling nostrils.
It will shoot blue flames from its sizzling tonsils.
And it will **ROAR!**

We've got to save the village,
we've got to save the planet.
We'll take a jar of Dragon's Breath.*
It cannot harm us ... can it?

(*Granny's Hot Chilli Chutney)

WE'RE OFF TO FEED THE DRAGON!

Ready, steady, go …
Left, right, left, right, left, right, left, right … STOP!
It's a bubbly, squidgy, gurgly, ever-so-stinky, boggy BOG.

Splodge, squelch, splodge, squelch, splodge, squelch, splodge …
Phew!

WE'RE OFF TO FEED THE DRAGON!

Ready, steady, go …
Left, right, left, right, left, right, left, right … STOP!
It's a bubbly, squidgy, gurgly, ever-so-pongy POND.

Plop, splosh, plop, splosh, plop, splosh, plop … Phew!

WE'RE OFF TO FEED THE DRAGON!

Ready, steady, go …
Left, right, left, right, left, right, left, right …
STOP!
It's a bubbly, squidgy, gurgly, ever-so-slippy, sloppy SWAMP.

Flump, slunch, flump, slunch, flump, slunch, flump …
Phew!

Shshsh ...
There's a
  rumbly, grumbly,
    croaky, smoky,
      ever-so choky,
        howly, growly
                ROAR
from the top of the mountain.
Is it a volcano? Is it a tornado?

No ... It's the DRAGON!

From boggy bogs and pongy ponds,
we've splashed through sploshy splodges.
We've splashed through slippy, sloppy swamps.
We've splashed through stinky stodges.

But now we're climbing Dragon Mountain …
Getting colder … darker … steeper.
The dragon is waiting!
It will puff red smoke from its sizzling nostrils.
It will shoot blue flames from its sizzling tonsils.
And it will **ROAR!**
We'll all be cooked to a frazzle …

We've got to climb the mountain;
we've got to reach the summit.
Don't slip your shoe in the dragon poo
or you'll stumble and tumble and plummet!

WE'RE OFF TO FEED THE DRAGON!

Ready, steady, go …
Left, right, left, right, left, right, left, right … STOP!
Oh no! It's a wibbly wobbly bridge dangling over a deep, dark, dangerous drop.

Wibble, wobble, wooaaah!
Wibble, wobble, wooaaah!
Phew!

WE'RE OFF TO FEED THE DRAGON!

Ready, steady, go …
Left, right, left, right, left, right, left, right …
STOP!
Oh no! It's a slippy, drippy cliff.

Grip, slip, wooaaah! Grip, slip, wooaaah!
Phew!

WE'RE OFF TO FEED THE DRAGON!

Ready, steady, go …
Left, right, left, right, left, right, left, right … STOP!
Oh no! It's a jagged ledge with a jagged edge – crumbly, tumbly, ever-so-fumbly.

Crumble, fumble, wooaaah!
Crumble, fumble, wooaaah!
Phew!

Shshsh …
Up on that rock are scaly things:
a scaly tail and scaly wings,
and scaly legs with savage claws;
a scaly head with fiery jaws.

We'll have to take it by surprise.
Quick, hide from those big staring eyes.
It's already seen us!
It puffs red smoke from its sizzling nostrils.
It shoots blue flames from its sizzling tonsils.
And it **ROARS!**

Throw it a jar of Granny's Hot Chilli Chutney.

The dragon opens the chutney jar,
bites off the lid – away it's flung.
It sniffs inside, where pickles are
and licks a lick with a long green tongue …
And it **ROARS!**

Flames flare and glare,
blaze and dazzle,
sizzle and frazzle.
Run home quick – it's time to skedaddle …

Back across the jagged ledge with the crumbly, fumbly, jagged edge …
Crumble, fumble, wooaaah!
Crumble, fumble, wooaaah!

Back right down the slippy cliff, the drippy slippy iffy cliff …
Grip, slip, wooaaah!
Grip, slip, wooaaah!

Back across the wobbly bridge, the wibbly wobbly knobbly bridge
Wibble, wobble, wooaaah!
Wibble, wobble, wooaaah!

Back through the sloppy swamp …
Flump, slunch, flump, slunch, flump, slunch, flump.

Back through the pongy pond …
Plop, splosh, plop, splosh, plop, splosh, plop.

Back through the boggy bog …
Splodge, squelch, splodge, squelch, splodge, squelch, splodge.

And we're home!

Shshsh …
Did you hear that noise?
There's something in the kitchen.

Something hot and fiery;
something hot and noisy;
something hot and steamy.
Open the door very slowly and take a tiny peep …
Is it the d- d- dragon?

It's Granny!
"Welcome home, you silly-billy.
While you've been hiking where it's hilly,
I've made pickles willy-nilly!
New SIZZLY chilli piccalilli."

Please note:
No dragons were harmed in the telling of this story.